The Water Princess

A Classic Adventure

A
Classic
Adventure

THE WATER PRINCESS

By
Ron Ricci

The Water Princess: A Classic Adventure

Published by Gatekeeper Press
2167 Stringtown Rd, Suite 109
Columbus, OH 43123-2989
www.GatekeeperPress.com

ISBN (paperback): 9781642372878
eISBN: 9781642372885

Printed in the United States of America

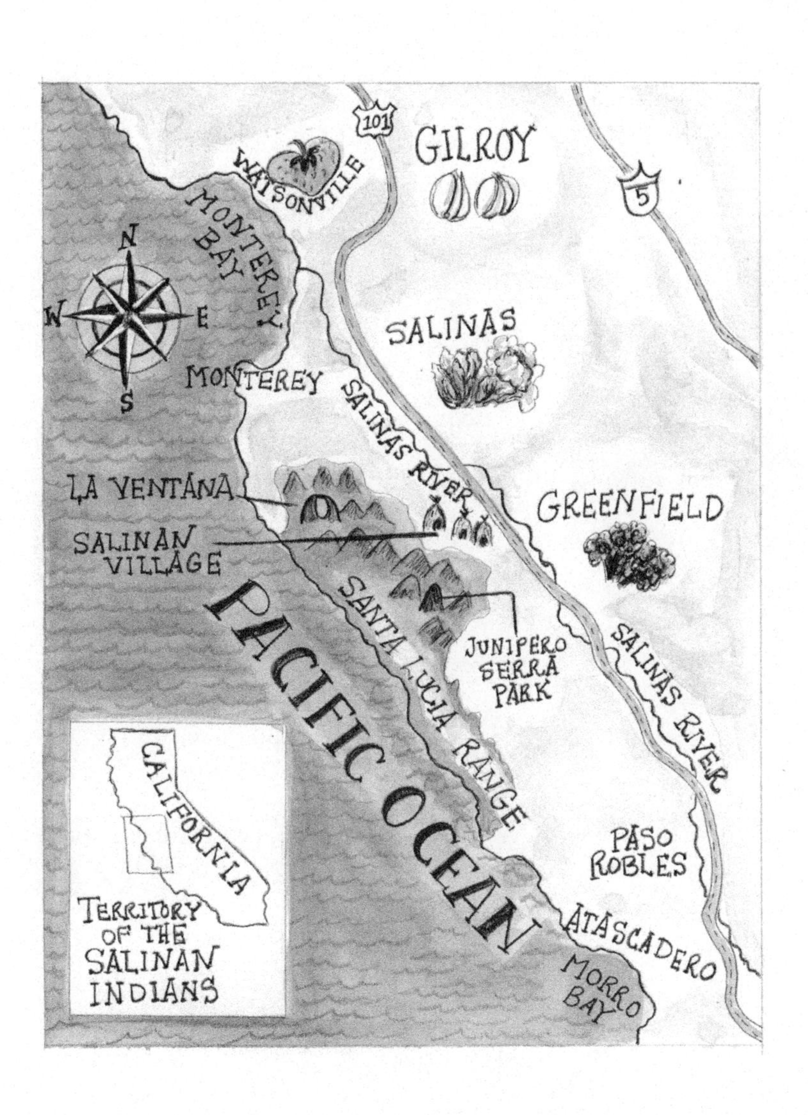
101
GILROY
5
WATSONVILLE
MONTEREY BAY
N
W
E
S
SALINAS
MONTEREY
SALINAS RIVER
LA VENTANA
GREENFIELD
SALINAN VILLAGE
PACIFIC OCEAN
SANTA LUCIA RANGE
JUNIPERO SERRA PARK
SALINAS RIVER
CALIFORNIA
PASO ROBLES
TERRITORY OF THE SALINAN INDIANS
ATASCADERO
MORRO BAY

“Sport, it’s time to leave,” he said. “Grab your sleeping bag and let’s head out.”

“I’m ready, Dad,” said eleven-year-old Casey.

“It’s a short drive before we get to the trail-head,” her father said. “Then we have a two-hour hike up to the campsite.”

“Do you think we have enough food?” she asked.

“I know you are only eleven, but you love food more than anyone I know!”

"It's your fault, Dad," Casey insisted.

"How so?" he asked.

"Look around," she twisted about. "We live on a farm."

"I guess you're right," he laughed. "Our dinner table never lacks vegetables or fruit."

"Maybe we can we stop to get some strawberries for tonight?" she asked.

"Let's get some on the way home," he suggested. "We can visit one of fruit stands near Salinas."

"It's November. Do you think they'll still be sweet?"

"Of course, they will!" he said excitedly. "We're just a short drive to the Strawberry Capital of the World."

"Dad, it seems like we have a lot of capitals around here."

"What do you mean?"

"Well, whenever we drive on highway 101, I see a sign welcoming people to 'Gilroy, the Garlic Capital of the World.' Down the road, Salinas claims they're the lettuce capital. Greenfield is broccoli. And Watsonville swears they're the strawberry capital."

"It's all true. If the Salinas Valley were the only country in the world, no one would go hungry."

"Wow," she wondered. "I wish that were true."

"It's a unique place," he looked around proudly. "We're lucky to live here."

"Casey, do you remember when your brother acted in the school play last year?"

"When everyone dressed up like Abraham Lincoln?" she asked.

"That's right; even the girls had beards," he laughed. "Do you remember when the class recited the poem, 'America the Beautiful'?"

"I remember; a couple of the beards started to fall off, and a bunch of the kids started laughing!" she cackled.

"I forgot about that," he chuckled. "It's a beautiful poem about our country."

"Where's this going, Dad?"

"There's a verse in the poem that describes the American countryside with the words 'amber waves of grain,'" he said the final words slowly.

"I remember," she said.

"Look around," he waved his hand across the car's dashboard. "Everything is the color of 'amber waves of grain.'"

"It's beautiful, Dad."

"That's what this trip is about," he told her. "It's why we're here."

"We do enough work at home," she smiled. "I hope you're not asking me to pick some of those amber waves of grain."

"These hills may be amber today, but they will be as green as Ireland in a month's time."

"That's fast—like magic," she said.

"It is magic," he agreed. "Only a few places in the world have the same climate as we do. The Salinas valley is very special."

"Does this have anything to do with this camping trip?" she asked.

"Everything," he said emphatically. "It's

mid-November, about the halfway point between fall and winter. The time of the year when our rainy season begins."

"We're camping because of the rain?" she asked. "You always told us it wasn't fun to camp when the ground is wet."

"The water," he replied as he put his hand on her shoulder.

"Right," she said slowly, and paused before whispering, "the water."

And then she added, as if she were talking to herself, "And the waters will show us the way."

"You remembered," he smiled. "I'm proud of you."

"You have the map on your phone, Casey?"

"Got it," she said. "GPS says about thirty-seven more minutes before we turn west and locate our base camp on the peak."

"You sound like a pilot announcing landing."

"Roger, we should be there in fifty-eight minutes at this pace," she mimicked a pilot talking on a microphone.

"I know the signs say this is the trail to Junipero Serra Peak," he said, "but a hundred years ago, people walking right here would have called this the Pimkolam Peak Trail."

"That's hard to say."

"I agree; it is difficult to pronounce," he said before he stopped walking, bent down and pointed. "Look at this."

"What is it?" she said, looking over his shoulder as he bent down.

"This plant is in the salvia family —or at least that is what these plants are called by botanists."

"It's everywhere, Dad," she noted as she scanned the nearby canyons.

"People cook with salvia all the time," he added. "In grocery stores, it's called sage."

"There is so much here you could cook forever," she said.

"This is a special kind of salvia," he said. "The Native Americans who lived here before the Europeans arrived called this plant pimkolam; that's why this was once called the trail to Pimkolam Peak."

"That's cool to know," she said.

"It's just the beginning of how cool pimkolam can be, as you'll soon find out," he said quickly and left her kneeling and looking out at the hills and canyons in her own thoughts.

"Wow, look at the time. It must be getting close to sunset. What do you think, Dad?"

"I know," he chuckled. "I promised dinner before sundown!"

"Just sayin'. You know how grumpy I get when I'm hungry!" Casey laughed.

"Trust me," he looked at her, "I know, but I'm well-prepared. You won't starve."

"How prepared?" She put her hands on her hips and pretended to be mad.

"I brought one of the briskets you love so

much. You know, from one of the ranches south of Gilroy," he smiled.

"What are we waiting for? Let's get the fire going!" she shouted, raising her arms in the air.

"If you had to guess," he said, standing up, "which side of this peak is going to have the most deadwood for our fire pit?"

"The canyons on this side of the mountain are mostly amber," she said, looking around. "But the Pacific side of the peak is greener."

"I know I don't need to tell you where the firewood is, do I?"

"The east side, of course." She pointed to the drier, amber canyons.

"Let's get to work," Dad said.

"It seems weird," she said while glancing from from side to side as they walked.

"What do you mean, Casey?"

"From here, we can see both sides of the mountain. The colors are so different."

"I know," he said. "Let's hope the rain comes soon."

"I bet I can fill my arms faster than you can

with firewood," she said suddenly and quickly started gathering smaller kindling wood.

"I'll take the challenge!" He rushed about, picking up heavier pieces of wood.

"I win!" Casey yelled out. The two of them laughed and started walking back to the campsite.

"How's your Spanish coming along, young lady?" he asked.

"Got an A, Dad," she said. "You know that."

"Well, what does the Spanish word 'ventana' mean?" he asked.

"Window," she answered.

"Welcome to the Ventana Wilderness," he

said.

"If I've got my Spanish right, what does the 'window wilderness' mean?" she asked.

"It's a metaphor." He stopped walking. "Not a description."

"What does that mean? What's a metaphor?"

They arrived at the campsite and put the firewood and kindling down.

"Look in that direction." He pointed toward two mountain peaks separated by a large open notch between them.

"There's a huge hole between those two mountains," she said, her eyes widening at the size of the opening.

"That hole is what the Spanish called 'La Ventana;' literally, a window with a view of the Pacific Ocean."

"To be a window, it would need a frame," she noted.

"True," he answered. "But what if I told you legend has it there once was a frame?"

"That would mean some kind of bridge or path linked the two peaks," she wondered and unconsciously moved her hand across the horizon where the path would have been.

"Exactly," he said.

"The ventana would have been spectacular," she said excitedly. "You could see right through it."

"Do you think the legend is true?" he asked. "Do you think a bridge was there?"

"I do," she said confidently, not really knowing why.

"So do I," he nodded in agreement. "But I think the Spanish were right and wrong at the same time."

"What do you mean, Dad?"

"I think the Spanish were right to name this area La Ventana – the window," he said. "But I think they got their geography wrong."

"I didn't bring a topology map, Dad," she smiled.

"You can look through a window from two sides, depending on where you're standing — it's a matter of perspective," he explained. "One side of La Ventana would have looked west out to the Pacific; but if you stood on the other side, you would look east."

"I don't need a compass to tell me we are looking through the 'east window' right now," she said, "because the sun is setting to the west behind us."

"Right, 'la ventana del este'—the window to the east—would have looked toward our home and the Salinas Valley, in this direction." He stopped talking and just looked toward the hills and the valleys in the distance with his back to the ocean.

"This is all very interesting and educational," she said after a few seconds. "But how 'bout we get the fire going for that brisket?"

"That was some of the best brisket ever!" Casey said as she looked up from her plate

"It was good," Dad nodded emphatically. "We worked up quite an appetite this afternoon."

"So, are you finally going to tell me why we are here?" she asked.

"I am – and you already know it has something to do with water," he told her.

"Yes, the water," she said.

"Do you remember a few years back when

we had the El Niño winter and it rained so much?" he asked.

"Our backyard flooded, I remember."

"That's right – you've got a good memory," he said. "Because of the drought, most of the creeks on our farm were dry, which is why we started calling them by their Spanish name: the 'arroyo seco,' the dry creek."

"It's Saturday night, Dad, not Monday in school." She smiled at him.

"OK, I'll lay off the Spanish lesson – you remember that the largest creek on our farm overflowed and spilled into our yard?"

"We were all afraid the house would float away!" she said anxiously.

"The flash floods were so strong," he continued, "that they turned up a lot of stones on the creek bed that hadn't been moved for decades, maybe centuries. That's where I found this." He pulled a stone from his pocket and handed it to her.

"It's an arrowhead," she said right away.

"It's no ordinary arrowhead."

"What do you mean?" she asked.

"Look closely; turn it over."

"I see some scratches, like someone tried to carve lines on it."

"What do the scratches look like?" he asked.

"It can't be," she stopped, and looked up at him sharply. "It looks like a window."

"La Ventana," he said.

"Dad, I might be eleven, but I know the Salinan Indians didn't speak Spanish."

"They didn't – but maybe the Spanish didn't imagine La Ventana," he told her.

"I don't think the Indians had ever heard of a window, Dad."

"I'm sure you're right," he said. "But maybe, the Spanish got the idea for the La Ventana from stories they heard from the Salinan Indians."

"Wow," she said. "I wonder if that really

happened?"

"I think it did," he told her.

"What makes you think so?" she wanted to know.

"Because of a story I heard when I was your age," he said. "When I went camping with Grandpa Al."

"Tell me," she said.

"You know, of course, that Grandpa was one of the pioneers of organic vegetable farming in the Salinas Valley," he said.

"Everyone knows that," she said with a smile.

"And you know Grandpa had a foreman named Hector," he added.

"Grandpa gave him some land to thank him for his help starting our farm," she said.

"Some of Hector's family still live there today and continue to grow artichokes on the land," he said.

"So what story did you hear?" she wanted to know.

"Grandpa brought Hector camping with us," he said. "And Hector told us the most spectacular story over a campfire just like this one."

"What was the story called?" she asked.

"It's why we are here," he said. "It's your turn to hear the story."

"What's it called?" she asked again.

"The Water Princess."

PART TWO

"I am not well, Daughter."

"I know, Father. Drink this. The hot water will ease your pain and the pimkolam will soothe your cough"

"You have learned your lessons well," he said, coughing.

"I have had the best teacher," she smiled reluctantly, tipping the cup to his lips.

"Our people are thirsty and hungry," he whispered.

"We are all weak." She looked down the mountain trails at the deserted structures.

"I have taught you to cook with pimkolam

to heal our sick and keep our people growing," he said.

"You are the keeper of the ancient ways we use to prepare our food and make our water strong," she reminded him, trying to stay positive.

"Without water, there is no food, Daughter," he said.

"It will rain soon," she said.

"It must, but it hasn't." He gestured and pointed toward the canyons.

"The hills are the color of the sun everywhere now," she said.

"When there is only one color, there is no life," he said the words slowly.

"There is only one left whose color is different, Father."

"You understand the truth, as I do." He started to weep as he said the words.

"Only one pimkolam plant remains," she agonized, knowing the meaning of the words.

"You have kept it alive?" he asked.

"I have."

"You have been leaving every day at sunrise?" he asked. "You have gone to the ancient spring I showed you to bring water to the pimkolam and me?"

"I have, but I have not found water in five sunrises," she answered.

"The ancient spring no longer flows?" he asked sadly.

"I have cleared the stones and dug deeper, but the water has disappeared into the earth," she said.

"This pimkolam is very old, Daughter." He turned to the plant.

"The leaves are still good for cooking, but tired of the struggle without water," she despaired.

"Soon the leaves will be the same color as the hills," he told her.

"No . . . ." Her voice trailed off into a whisper.

"Everything we are as a people can be found in this plant," he said.

"It gives us healing powers when we are sick, and it makes our food taste better, too," she said.

“When it rained and we could grow squash and beans, the pimkolam always made our food taste better,” he laughed.

“Pimkolam in hot water always makes our throats feel better, especially when there were bees and we could find honey to make it sweet,” she said.

“Let’s not forget that pimkolam helps our elders remember where we put things,” he added with a small laugh.

“The plant gives more than it takes,” she said with a smile.

“Give more than you take,” he joined her with a smile.

“It has showed us the way,” the daughter told her father.

“It has showed us the way,” her father repeated.

"Tonight, the moon will not appear," he told her. "I want you to go hunting when it is darkest."

"There are no animals left, Father."

"I do not want you to hunt for animals, Daughter," he said.

"Why am I hunting in the dark for nothing at all?"

"I want you to hunt near the star that stands still," he told her.

"We have looked at the star many times,

but I have never seen anything in the night sky that I could hunt. How can I hunt for something I cannot see?" she asked.

"You won't; the pimkolam will do the hunting," his voice changed to the tone when he taught her to cook the ancient recipes.

"How will this plant reach the sky?" she wanted to know.

"It cannot, but you can help it," he said.

"I am not tall enough."

"You can get the pimkolam to the star if you use your bow and arrow," he instructed her.

"I will get it," she said immediately.

"Not yet," he stopped her. "Our arrow must be made with root of this pimkolam."

"But it is the last one," she hesitated.

"Yes," he interrupted, "the last pimkolam will give more than it takes – one final time."

"If I must do this and take this plant from its home in the ground, you must tell me why, Father."

"The pimkolam will show us the way," he said.

"It has always shown us the way," she retorted.

"Tonight, it will show us the way to the water."

"The arrow is finished," she showed him.

"It is beautiful," he said.

"The root is very strong," she said.

"Do you know what is inside?" He asked.

"The root is from a pimkolam plant. Pimkolam must be inside," she deduced.

"This root contains the seeds of our future," he told her.

"How can we plant seeds with this Pimkolam arrow if I'm hunting in the night sky?" she wanted to know.

"You are going to attach this arrowhead to it." He handed her a clover stone.

"What are these markings on the arrowhead?" she asked.

"Look closely," he said.

"I see the path between the two peaks," she answered, looking up in surprise.

"The arrowhead is made from the stone found on the path," he told her.

"It is as beautiful as the pimkolam wood," she observed.

"Once the arrow is complete, we are going to the peak closest to the ocean," he told her.

"We will shoot the arrow from the path?" she asked.

He nodded. "The sea wind will be at our back and help guide the arrow to its target," he said.

"The star that stands still is always the brightest in the sky," she remembered.

"We will plant the seeds near the star that

stands still," he said.

"And the water?" she asked.

"The pimkolam wood is behind an arrowhead made from the path's stone; that gives me hope for our people, for our land," he finished.

"The path is as old as our people," he reminded her.

"Are the ancient stories true?" she asked.

"I believe them. Do you?" he asked.

"I do believe that the path between the two peaks was built by people," she said, looking at the path.

"It is difficult to imagine anyone or anything other than people could have built the path," he mused.

"The stories say our people have been here since the path appeared."

"Before the path, it was a dark time for the people living here," he reminded her.

"It is difficult to imagine how this arrow will reach the sky or find water." She changed the subject.

"It is again a dark time," he said in his teaching voice.

"How can this possibly work?" she wondered. "How will this single arrow find the water we need from the night sky?"

"I am sure the brothers who built this path said the same thing in their darkest nights," he said in a calm voice.

"What do you think the brothers were thinking?" she asked him. "What would they tell their sister?"

"It would be simple," he said.

"What?"

"If you have given, then you will be given." He smiled as he put his hand on her shoulder.

"You are saying I have to believe I can do it," she concluded.

"The future of our people depends on it." He looked at her both as a teacher and as a father.

"But the brothers who built this path did not give more than they took," she emphasized.

"You remember the ancient story well," he said.

"Each of the brothers wanted to win their father's favor so that when their father died, he would grant all of his land to only one of them," she repeated from memory.

"The two brothers," he continued, "each raced to build the tallest peak in the valley to impress him.

"Using their own hands and many seasons of digging and moving earth, they created the peaks we see before us." Father gestured toward them.

"The amount of rock and dirt they moved to build these peaks disturbed the earth," she said.

"The brothers kept building the peaks higher and higher," he added as he closed his eyes. "They dug so deeply into the surrounding valleys that the earth weakened and started to move violently all the time."

"The shaking of the earth must have been terrifying to the people who lived here," she shuddered.

"When the father eventually died, there was no land left to claim," he said soberly.

"The people living here were dying from all the shaking," she said like an adult.

"The brothers built this path between the two peaks with the stones crushed by the moving earth," he said.

"When the final stone was laid in the path, the shaking suddenly stopped," she said.

"Instead of two competing peaks, there was one path between them," he said.

"The earth has not moved for as long as anyone remembers," she smiled.

"Our people have been here ever since," he finished.

"I am tired, Daughter, and my sickness is making it difficult to continue," he told her, coughing.

"Maybe tonight is not the night, Father."

"It must be tonight," he insisted. "And I believe you must do it alone."

"Why must this be the night?" she questioned him. "Why not tomorrow?"

"Tomorrow, the moon will return. It will be harder for you to hunt," he said.

"Why does that matter?"

"Because the light from the moon will confuse your arrow and make it more difficult to find its target," he said in a calm voice.

"I will and can do it tonight," she affirmed.

"The markings on the arrowhead stop near the middle of the path, but closer to the peak opposite the ocean." He looked out at the long path in the dark night. "It is too far for me to walk; I will only hold you back."

"Where will I aim, Father?" she asked.

"Let me tell you what I once heard from the elders in the sweat lodge: Near the star that stands still, there are four stars that form a bowl," he said, pointing to an area of the night sky.

"I see them and the bowl they form," she said.

"A visitor from another people told us the bowl holds a special power." He continued to describe what he had heard in the lodge. "They said the power had the ability to save—or destroy—our land."

"I cannot see anything," she said.

"They said it could not be seen."

"What does this have to do with water?" she

asked.

"Our land—our people need to be saved. I believe water is inside the bowl," he told her.

"The arrow will pierce the bowl and release the water. It will fill the sky with rain," she immediately understood.

"The pimkolam will show you the way, Daughter."

"I am ready," she said.

"I will wait here," he said.

"I will shoot the way you taught me," she said, looking at him.

"You are a better hunter than me," he smiled as his eyes filled with tears.

"Tonight, I am hunting for you, Father." She started to cry.

"For us all," he said.

"For us all."

"Hold the arrow with me," his voice firmed.

"Let us hold it together." She wrapped her arms around the arrow and her father.

"If you believe you have given," he whispered in her ear, "you will be given."

“I am your daughter!” she cried out suddenly, grabbing the arrow from him and running down the path holding her bow in one hand and the Pimkolam arrow in the other.

“I am your father!” he yelled, watching as she vanished into the night.

"As important as this arrow is, the bow is just as important to reach the bowl of four stars," she said to herself. "The sea wind will be at my back, helping with the flight of the arrow, as Father said."

She continued down the path, running as fast as she could. "My bow is made of the yew tree, and I know it is the strongest," she remembered.

"The yew wood will bend and release tremendous energy to power my arrow's flight," she assured herself.

"I am where I am supposed to be, and it is time." She stopped running, remembering the arrowhead carvings. "I will calm my breathing and let my heart slow so I can steady my aim."

I cannot see Father, she thought, turning back to look down the path toward the ocean. I can see the other end of the path when I look toward my target, she noted in her mind.

"I am certain I am where I need to be. I am going to aim for the heart of the bowl—where I believe the water is," she said. "This arrow will save our people."

She pulled the drawstring back slowly and deliberately while she arched her back and bent her legs. "This arrowhead brings with it the strength of the path." She steadied her aim.

"This ocean wind is my friend," she whispered as the breeze from the ocean strengthened at her back.

"The pimkolam has given and I know it will give again!" she yelled as the arrow released into the night sky – its path visible in the starlight and in the ocean mist, leaving the arc of a trail behind it. As soon as the arrow reached the night sky, she immediately felt the stones beneath her feet move; she suddenly realized the path between the two peaks was beginning to crumble.

"Dad! Why did you stop?" Casey said, exasperated when he suddenly got quiet and stood up in front of her.

"Sorry, Sport, but to find out what happened to the Water Princess and her father, we need to know what happened to the Pimkolam arrow," he told her.

"Whatever it takes!" She raised her voice like an excited kid opening presents at a birthday party.

"To help me finish the story, I'd like you to come over here and bring the arrowhead," he asked.

"OK, but will you tell me what happened?" she pleaded.

"Of course, but stand here and hold the arrowhead in front of you." He gestured to where he wanted her to position herself so she could see the two peaks that formed La Ventana. "Using the arrowhead's map as a guide, try to imagine where the Water Princess stood when she shot her arrow on the path between the two peaks."

"She would have been about here," she said, using her right hand to hold the arrowhead in front of her face and her left hand to point toward La Ventana.

"OK. If she was standing there, where is the star that stands still?" he asked.

"Well, I know the Salinan Indians called the North Star by that name," she recalled, still holding her left hand where she believed the Water Princess stood on the path between the two peaks.

"That's right. Explorers in the Northern Hemisphere guided themselves by what's called the North Star," he told her. "While other stars changed position as the earth rotated and circled the sun, the North Star appeared to 'stand still.'"

"So, she would have shot the arrow from here," she decided, pointing with her left hand between the two peaks. "But she would have aimed with her back to the ocean and into the north sky," she motioned her right hand toward the North Star.

"That's right; now, where is the bowl of four stars?" he asked her.

"Well, directly next to the North Star, I see the Little Dipper and then there's the . . . . Wait! Are you kidding me, Dad?" She instantly understood.

"Tell me what you see and what you think." Casey's dad wanted her to say out loud what her mind was telling her.

"Four stars form a bowl directly below the Little Dipper," she said quickly.

"Yes . . . ." He waited for her to finish the

story, even though she had never heard it before.

"The Water Princess would have shot the Pimkolam arrow from here on the path between the two peaks," she summarized by gesturing with her left hand. "Of course, those two peaks are the mountains that form the imaginary 'window' that the Spanish named La Ventana. If she had been standing near the middle of the path—on what would have been the top side of La Ventana's window frame—the arrow would have shot north with the ocean wind helping it from the west, and judging from the angle of flight, the stone arrowhead would have struck the bowl of four stars on the top star of the bowl closest to where we are standing now!" she finished, speaking faster and pointing up and up and up with each successive thought.

"The Water Princess would have pierced the bowl with her arrow," he said.

"You can still see the arrow today," she said excitedly.

"The Pimkolam arrow shot by the Water

Princess is indeed still anchored to the bowl of four stars," he smiled.

"No one calls it 'the bowl of four stars' anymore, Dad," she teased him.

"That's what the people who lived in ancient times called it," he pointed out.

"That's not what people call it today," she insisted and put her hand on her hips.

"So, I've heard—" he smiled and then opened his mouth like he was about to say something.

"And that's how the Big Dipper was formed!" she screamed out before her father could.

"By piercing the bowl and forming the Big Dipper, the Pimkolam arrow with the stone arrowhead released the power trapped inside," she said.

"Whatever power it was, the bowl instantly burst, like a dam holding back a powerful river or a lake," he added.

"And it rained and rained." She smiled.

"And the hills turned green." He smiled back.

"The power that released the water from the

bowl must have destroyed the path between the two peaks," she hypothesized.

"Whatever was holding back the water had to be powerful," her dad agreed.

"The rain saved the Water Princess and her father." She closed her eyes as she said it.

"How do you know?" he asked.

"I'm holding in my hand what she held in hers," she said with her eyes still closed, gripping the stone arrowhead.

"Do you really believe that's possible?" he wanted to know.

"She did shoot the arrow north toward the Salinas Valley," she suggested.

"Maybe it dislodged from the arrow when it struck the bowl?" he wondered.

"Maybe it did," she agreed. "All I know is when I close my eyes I can see the two of them near a river and the riverbanks are filled with salvia, or pimkolam."

"What else do you see?" he asked.

"I can tell you the river runs south to north, because I can see the sun to the west of them," she said.

"Only one river runs south to north in this part of California," he said.

"I know," she opened her eyes.

"The Salinas River runs north from the watershed we're standing in right now and travels all the way to where we live and farm today," he told her.

"This must be her arrowhead," she said with all her heart.

EPILOGUE

"Daughter, I feel so much better." Her father looked younger and stronger and the Water Princess smiled.

"When I found you," she said, "Pimkolam was growing all over your body."

"The pimkolam saved my life and has given once more." He smiled.

"When the arrow struck the bowl with four stars, it started to rain immediately," she said. "Almost at the same time, the path between the two peaks collapsed."

"I am happy to be alive, and I am very happy you are alive," he said proudly. "But you have saved more than your father – you have saved our people."

"I am happy for our people, and I am happy for you." Her eyes watered.

"Remember when I told you the arrow contained the seeds of our future?" he asked.

"I do."

"When the Pimkolam arrow struck the bowl with four stars, it released the water trapped inside and a pimkolam seed must have been carried by every raindrop," he said, looking around at the fresh growth.

"This river is new, too, and the plant growth is everywhere," she observed.

"We can move our people to where the water is flowing or toward where the water started," he said, looking up and down the river.

"I wonder which way is better?" she mused.

"More pimkolam is growing in this direction," he motioned. "The farming must be better here."

"The pimkolam is following the river, and we will let the waters of the river show us the way to our new home." She smiled and started walking with the sun to her left and the river in front of her.

“Dad, I’ve got a question.”

“What’s up, Casey?” he answered.

“In the story, the father of the Water Princess said, ‘when there is no color except one, there is no life,’” she said.

“That’s right,” he agreed.

“Aren’t these hills all the same color?”

“It looks that way,” he said.

“The color is telling us something, Dad, but perhaps we’re not seeing it . . . yet.”

“It is showing us a way,” he agreed.

“We sometimes take more water from the

ground than is given to us from the skies," she said.

"Maybe we should try something different," he told her.

"Maybe we should," she agreed.

"We can still get strawberries near Salinas, if you want," he suggested.

"Yes!" she cried out. "Let's get them while we still can!"

STRAWBERRIES
FRESH
2.50

Made in the USA
Monee, IL
03 December 2020